This book belongs to

Don't Eat Pete!
An original concept by author Sue Walker
© Sue Walker
Illustrated by Carlo Beranek

MAVERICK ARTS PUBLISHING LTD
Studio 3A, City Business Centre, 6 Brighton Road, Horsham,
West Sussex, RH13 5BB, +44 (0)1403 256941
© Maverick Arts Publishing Limited
Published June 2019

A CIP catalogue record for this book
is available at the British Library.

ISBN 978-1-84886-426-9

www.maverickbooks.co.uk

DON'T EAT PETE!

Written by Sue Walker

Illustrated by Carlo Beranek

Dedicated to Pete, my inspiration – S.W.

For my Mom and Dad, the greatest heroes in the world – C.B.

Like most trolls, Uncle Boll loved his food.
He sometimes burped, but was rarely rude.
Being greedy was his biggest flaw,
He would eat and eat but still want more.

When Moll asked Boll to puppy-sit Pete,
She made certain there was lots to eat.
"I'm off to work," said Moll, "but please,
Help yourself to bread and cheese.

There's coleslaw, crackers, tins of meat,
But Uncle Boll, please DON'T EAT PETE!"

"Eat Pete?" said Uncle, "Why, that's absurd!
Please don't worry, I give you my word.

With my hand on my heart, I repeat,
Your good Uncle Boll, will NOT EAT PETE!"

Meeting Pete, Boll was taken aback,
Small and sweet, Pete would make a great snack.
He cuddled him, stroked him, took him outside,

Then sniffed him,
licked him
and opened up wide...

"No!" thought Boll, "he is not here to eat!"

Then he said out loud, "DO NOT EAT PETE!"

The biscuit tin was there on the shelf,
Boll took off the lid and helped himself.

Pete liked biscuits too but Boll was so mean,
He ate every one and licked the tin clean.

Then to the kitchen Boll went to look,
For something tasty that he could cook.

Moll had left a note on the fridge door:

Dear Uncle Boll, if you would like more,
You can make yourself a tasty snack,
But don't eat Pete before I get back.
Just

DON'T EAT PETE!

Pete sniffed bacon from under the grill,
It seemed Uncle Boll was hungry still.
He gave that troll a long, hard stare,
Surely now Uncle Boll would share.

No. Boll was greedy and ate it all up,
Then turned his gaze to the little pug pup.
"Pete! Pete! Good enough to eat!
But no," said Boll, "DO NOT EAT PETE!"

Pete's tummy rumbled. Would Moll bring food home?

Some mince or some chops, or even a bone?

A nice juicy steak, now that would be great.

Pete wasn't sure he'd be able to wait...

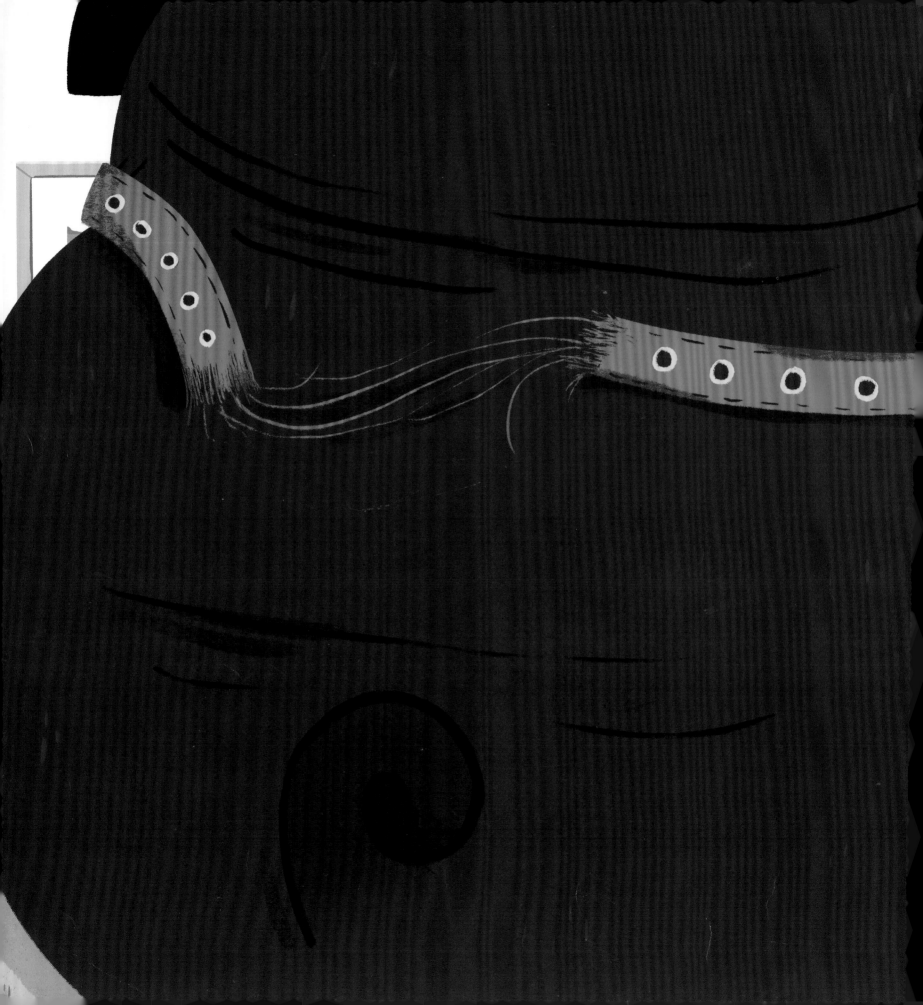

When Moll got home she said,
"Wow! Pete! You've grown!
How in two hours
have you put on ten stone?

BUUURRR

And where's Uncle Boll? Isn't he here?"
She looked confused, though it should have been clear.
Moll searched each room while Pete just looked on.
Only he knew where Uncle Boll had gone.

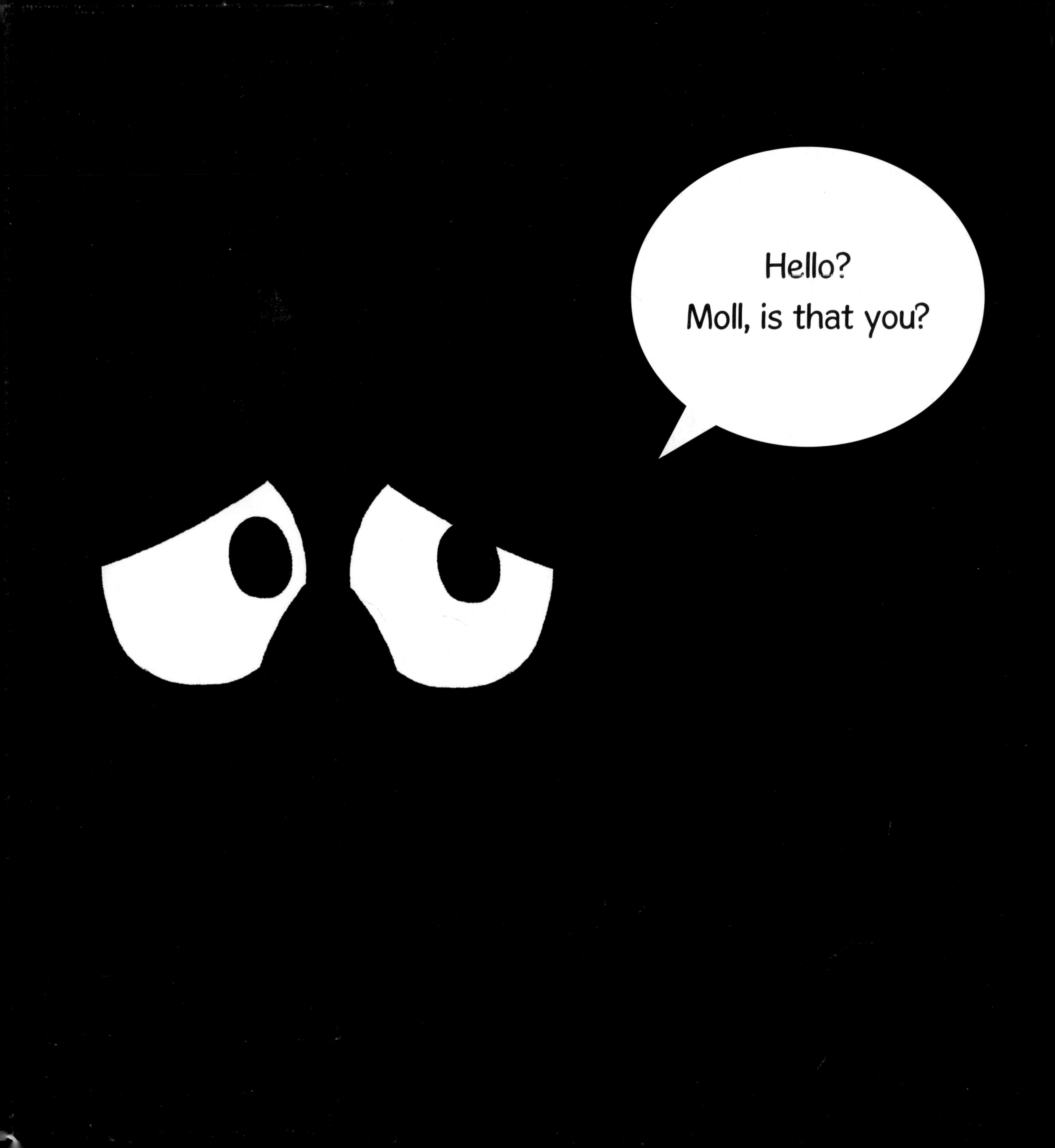
Hello?
Moll, is that you?